Two Places to Sleep

by Joan Schuchman

illustrations by
Jim LaMarche

CAROLRHODA BOOKS
MINNEAPOLIS, MINNESOTA USA

LIBRARY OF CONGRESS CATALOGING IN PUBLICATION DATA

Schuchman, Joan.
  Two places to sleep.

  SUMMARY: David describes living with his father and
visiting his mother on weekends after his parents' divorce.

  [1. Divorce—Fiction] I. LaMarche, Jim. II. Title.

PZ7.S385Mo   [E]   79-88201
ISBN 0-87614-108-4

4 5 6 7 8 9 10 99 98 97 96 95 94 93 92 91 90 89

to Jim and Lenny

My name is David. I'm seven. Some things I like are: sloppy Joes, baseball, talking with Mom on the phone. Here are some things I don't like: cleaning my room, taking out the garbage, Mom and Dad's divorce.

Mom lives in an apartment building in the city, and she works in an office downtown. Now when I come home from school, Mrs. Andrews is at our house. She's my dad's housekeeper, and she's nice. Sometimes I like to help her.

Mrs. Andrews says, "David, some things you can't change. You may not like them, but you just have to learn to live with them." She means the divorce. She's right about one thing—I don't like it.

Mrs. Andrews doesn't stay with us. She leaves when Dad gets home from work. Then Dad and I fix dinner. We are getting to be really good cooks. Friday night we made spaghetti.

Dad said, "You know, Davey, I really like to cook. I didn't think I would."

That reminded me of something. "Dad," I said, "my friend Tommy's parents are divorced, but he lives with his Mom. So does Peter. How come I live with you?"

Dad was frying hamburger. He said, "Remember when you and Mom and I met with Judge Thompson right before the divorce? Remember how we all decided that it would be better for you to stay where you've always lived?"

"I guess so," I said.

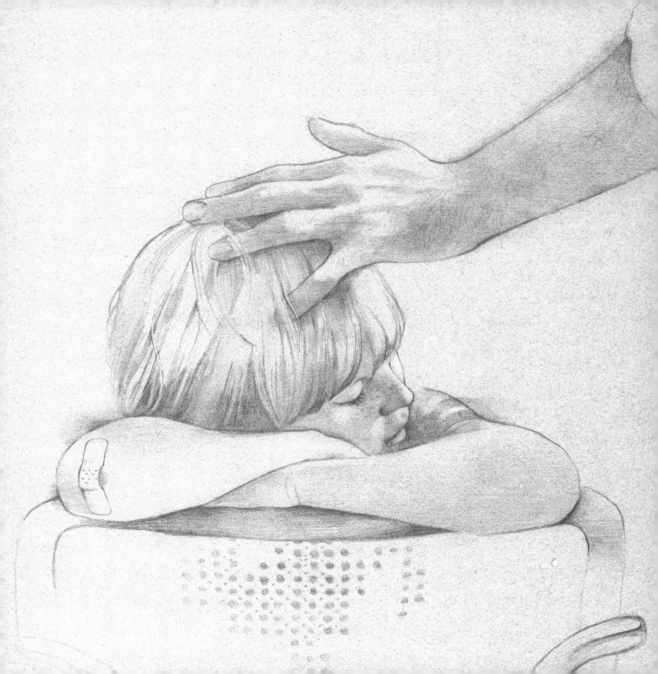

Dad turned off the stove. He sat down, and I sat on his lap. "Mom was moving into an apartment in the city," he said. "If you lived with her, you'd have to go to a different school and live in a strange neighborhood. It will take some time for you to get used to the divorce. You probably won't ever feel happy about it, but someday you won't feel so bad."

I wish it was Someday now.

Later on when I went to bed, Dad tucked me in. "Tomorrow's Saturday," he said. "You'll see your mom."

"I know," I said. "Good night, Dad."

"Sweet dreams, David," he said.

Saturday morning Dad fixed my very favorite breakfast, blueberry pancakes. They are one of his specialties.

"What are you going to do this weekend?" I asked him.

"Rake the leaves," he said. "Maybe I'll have time to finish building your bookcase too."

"Will you miss me?" I asked.

"Mmmhmm," he said. "But I know you'll be having a good time with Mom."

Just then we heard a car come into the driveway. It was Mom!

Mom gave me a big hug and kiss when I got into the car. She smelled so nice. I love the way my mom smells.

"I bought us a kite," she said.

"Oh, boy!" I said. "Can we fly it?"

Mom laughed. "That's what it's for," she said.

We went right to the park. There were a lot of children playing catch and flying kites. Peter was there with his dad.

"Peter is divorced too," I told Mom.

"No, David," she said. "Peter isn't divorced. Peter's *parents* are divorced. Moms and dads may get divorced from each other, but they never get divorced from their children."

"But you don't live with me any more," I told her.

"I know," she said, "and that makes me feel sad. But your dad and I can't live together any more. We don't get along."

"Sometimes you and I don't get along," I
told Mom.

"Most of the time we do," she said.
"Think of it this way. Your dad and I met
each other when we were twenty years old.
But we met you the very second you were
born. You're our own very special little boy.
We couldn't get a divorce from you, and
we would never want to. We both love
you very much, and we always will."

Suddenly she smiled. "Come on, let's
race," she said. We ran until we were out
of breath. Then we drove into the city to
her apartment.

While we ate lunch, I told her about everything that happened in school last week. "I got all my spelling words right for the third week in a row."

That made Mom happy. "What else happened last week?" she asked. She was really listening. She listens better now than she used to.

Later we went to the movies. We saw a show about a boy and his dog, and it made us laugh a lot. Then we went to a restaurant. I ordered my favorite dinner, fried chicken and a chocolate malt. Mom and I were eating and laughing and having a good time. Then I accidentally spilled my malt. Mom wasn't angry. She just wiped up the spill and ordered me another malt. But I couldn't stop thinking about my accident.

That night we played *Parcheesi* together until my bedtime. "Mom," I said, "if I'm very careful not to spill anything again and always clean up my room as soon as you ask, could you get undivorced from Dad?"

"I'm afraid not, David," she said. "You're not the reason for our divorce. Please try to understand that. We think you're wonderful just the way you are."

Mom read me a bedtime story. Then she kissed me good-night. "I love you, David," she said.

"I love you too, Mom," I told her. "I love you *and* Dad."

"And Daddy and I will always love you," she said.

Then she turned out the light. She left the door open a little, the way I like it, and I could hear her humming in the other room. It's sort of strange having two places to sleep now, one at Mom's apartment and one at home. At first I didn't like sleeping here, but now I'm getting used to it.

About the Author

JOAN SCHUCHMAN received her B.A. in English and Journalism from the University of Minnesota. She works as a freelance editor and writer, and has published book reviews, articles on scientific topics, and two paperbacks for Pamphlet Publications. Ms. Schuchman is the mother of two grown sons. She lives with her husband and their enormous dog in St. Paul, Minnesota.

About the Artist

JIM LAMARCHE's illustrations for his first book, MY DADDY DON'T GO TO WORK (Carolrhoda), were greeted with critical acclaim. "LaMarche's fine drawings portray loving humans who could belong to any race," said *Publishers Weekly*. The illustrations "are notable for their strong facial expressions that intensify the story's human concerns," added ALA *Booklist*. Mr. LaMarche received a degree in art from the University of Wisconsin in 1974, and now lives in Santa Cruz, California. This is his second book.